JE

How Mr. Monkey Saw the Whole World

Walter Dean Myers
Paintings by Synthia Saint James

A Picture Yearling Book

Published by
Bantam Doubleday Dell Books for Young Readers
a division of
Bantam Doubleday Dell Publishing Group, Inc.
1540 Broadway
New York, New York 10036

ISBN: 0-440-41415-6
Reprinted by arrangement with Doubleday Books for Young Readers

Printed in the United States of America

October 1997
10 9 8 7 6 5 4 3 2 1

For Hattie, Rose, Willie, Goldie, Alicia, and Lena
and all the other universal mothers
and the children they nurture

—S.S.J.

A very long time ago, before you were born, there was a small island on which Mr. Monkey lived. Mr. Monkey liked living there, and he walked around with his nose in the air and a flower in his hair. But then the famine came, and everybody had to work very hard just to find something to eat. Everybody, that is, but Mr. Buzzard.

One day, Mr. Monkey saw Mr. Buzzard talking to Mr. Hare. "Give me one yam for my belly," Mr. Buzzard said, "and I will fly you up to the clouds. You will be the first hare to see the whole world."

Mr. Hare knew that the yams he had were to feed himself and his family, but he had never seen the whole world before.

"I will give you one yam," Mr. Hare said.

So Mr. Buzzard flapped his wings and flew Mr. Hare high into the sky. He flew higher than the trees, and higher than the mountains. Mr. Hare looked down and saw the whole world, and he was happy.

But then Mr. Buzzard turned himself over and began to fly upside down.

"Don't fly upside down, Buzzard Bird!" Mr. Hare called out. "I will fall off!"

"If you give me ten yams," Mr. Buzzard said, "I will take you down safely."

Mr. Hare only had ten yams. But when he looked down and saw that the ground was so far away, he knew he was in big trouble. His heart was pounding like a drum.

"I will give you ten yams," Mr. Hare said.

When Mr. Buzzard heard this, he smiled a big buzzard smile. Then he turned himself right side up and flew to the ground. He took Mr. Hare's last ten yams and carried them to his house.

When Mr. Monkey saw this he was very mad.
His eyes grew shiny, and he gritted his teeth.
   "That was a bad thing to do to Mr.
Hare!" Mr. Monkey called out.
   But Mr. Buzzard did not care.
He sat by a wide baobab tree,
ate one of Mr. Hare's yams,
and grinned at the sun.

A week went by, and Mr. Buzzard was still not working. Mr. Hare was as skinny as a stick and walked around with a big tear in his eye.

Mr. Monkey saw Mr. Buzzard talking to Mr. Antelope.

"Give me one cassava root," Mr. Buzzard said, "and I will fly you up to the clouds. You will be the first antelope to see the whole world."

Mr. Antelope looked at his wife. She did not look too hungry, so he gave a cassava root to Mr. Buzzard.

Mr. Buzzard flew Mr. Antelope high into the
clouds. Mr. Antelope looked down and saw the
whole world.

"Oh, the world is such a beautiful place," Mr.
Antelope said.

But then Mr. Buzzard turned over and flew
upside down.

"Do not fly upside down, Mr. Buzzard!"
Mr. Antelope's eyes rolled around. "I will fall off!"

"If you give me twenty cassava roots," Mr.
Buzzard said, "I will fly you down safely."

Now, Mr. Antelope had only twenty roots. But
he looked down and knew he was in a lot of
trouble.

"I will give you the roots," Mr. Antelope said.
"Take me down."

Mr. Buzzard smiled as he straightened up, and he smiled as he flew Mr. Antelope down to the ground. He smiled even more as he took Mr. Antelope's roots.

Mr. Monkey saw this and did not like what he saw. He turned around three times and stamped his foot on the ground. "Why did you do that bad thing?" Mr. Monkey called to Mr. Buzzard.

But Mr. Buzzard did not listen. He just sat by the baobab tree, a juicy root dangling from his buzzard beak, and grinned at the sun.

Another month went by, and Mr. Buzzard was still not working. Mr. Antelope got skinny as a bone, and his wife ran away with a goat.

Then Mr. Monkey saw
Mr. Buzzard talking with Mr. Crab.

"If you give me one fish," Mr. Buzzard said,
"I will take you all the way up to the clouds. You
will be the first crab to see the whole world."

Mr. Crab knew he had only one fish to feed himself
and his family. But he wanted to be the first crab to
see the whole world. He gave Mr. Buzzard the fish.

Mr. Buzzard flew Mr. Crab high into the clouds. Mr.
Crab looked down and saw the whole world. He liked
seeing the whole world and smiled a smile that went
all the way around his head.

But then Mr. Buzzard turned upside down as he had before.

"Do not fly upside down, Mr. Buzzard!" Mr. Crab called out. "I am afraid!"

"If you give me forty fish," Mr. Buzzard said, "I will fly you down safely."

Mr. Crab covered his eyes and promised he'd catch forty fish to give Mr. Buzzard.

Two more months went by, and Mr. Buzzard was still not working. Mr. Buzzard looked up and saw Mr. Monkey sitting in a tree.

"Hey, Mr. Monkey!" Mr. Buzzard called out.

"What do you want, Mr. Buzzard?" Mr. Monkey said.

"If you give me one banana," Mr. Buzzard said, "I will fly you up to the clouds. You will be the first monkey to see the whole world."

Mr. Monkey thought quickly. He knew Mr. Buzzard had a rock where his heart should have been. Then he squeezed his face into a smile.

"I will give you one banana," Mr. Monkey said. "But first I have to get a palm leaf to keep the sun away from my head."

Mr. Monkey got the palm leaf, jumped onto
Mr. Buzzard's back, and held on as they flew to
the clouds.

Mr. Monkey saw the whole world for the first
time and smiled his best monkey smile and stuck
out his tongue.

Then Mr. Buzzard turned upside down.

Mr. Monkey was very scared. He held his breath
and wrapped his tail around Mr. Buzzard's neck.
Then he put the palm leaf over Mr. Buzzard's eyes.

"Turn me loose, Mr. Monkey!" Mr. Buzzard cried
out. "Take the leaf from my eyes!"

"No-noooo," Mr. Monkey said. "If you turn over
and fly right and give back the food you have
taken from Mr. Hare, Mr. Antelope, and Mr. Crab,
then I will let you fly down safely."

Mr. Buzzard was so mad!
He flew this way and that way,
and that way and this way,
but still Mr. Monkey held on.
Mr. Buzzard twirled and whirled
and flipped and dipped,
but it was no use.
Mr. Monkey had him.

Mr. Buzzard promised to give back the food he had left. Then Mr. Monkey took away the palm leaf from Mr. Buzzard's eyes. But he kept his tail wrapped around Mr. Buzzard's neck until they were down safely. Mr. Buzzard gave him the food and then flew away with an ugly look on his face.

Mr. Monkey called his friends Mr. Hare, Mr.
Antelope, and Mr. Crab, and they had a grand
party, dancing with their wives to calypso music
and talking about how beautiful the whole world
looked from the sky. Mr. Monkey ate as much as
he could and then laughed the loudest monkey
laugh that anybody on that island had ever heard.